18960771

WILLY IS MY BROTHER

Peggy Parish

Illustrated by Jacqueline Rogers

Delacorte Press

Published by
Delacorte Press
Bantam Doubleday Dell Publishing Group, Inc.
666 Fifth Avenue
New York, New York 10103

This edition is being published simultaneously in paperback
in a Young Yearling Book.

Text copyright © 1963, 1989 by Peggy Parish
Illustrations copyright © 1989 by Jacqueline Rogers

Library of Congress Cataloging in Publication Data
Parish, Peggy.
    Willy is my brother / by Peggy Parish; illustrated by
Jacqueline Rogers.
        p.   cm.
    Summary: A girl describes her love-hate relationship with
her brother Willy, who calls her a pest but comes to her
defense when another boy calls her the same thing.
    ISBN 0-385-29723-8
    [1. Brothers and sisters—Fiction.]   I. Rogers, Jackie, ill.
II. Title.
PZ7.P219Wi   1989
[E]—dc19
                                                88-34201
                                                    CIP
                                                     AC

Manufactured in the United States of America

May 1989

10 9 8 7 6 5 4 3 2 1

HR

For my brother, Stan—
The real Willy—
With love—

This story is about
Willy and me.
Willy is my brother.
He says I'm a pest, but he's really the
one who is a pest.

Last night at supper Willy got mad at me because I took the last cookie.

He said it was his.

He got so mad, he threw whipped cream at me.

He missed and I laughed.

But Daddy didn't laugh.
He sent us both away from the table.

We went upstairs to get ready for bed.

Willy went to his room and slammed the door.

I went to my room.

I put on my pajamas.

Then I crept over to Willy's room and opened the door very quietly.

I peeped in.

But Willy heard me and threw his pillow
at me. He was still mad.

I ran back to my room and got my pillow.

I crept up on Willy

and threw my pillow at him.
Bang—Bip—Bop!
We were having fun.
But then something happened.

"Whee, a feather storm!" shouted Willy.
Feathers flew everywhere.
We tried to catch them.
Willy wasn't mad anymore.

Then Mommy walked in.
Now SHE was mad.

I ran into my room and jumped into bed.

I don't know what Willy did.

His room was in a mess.

I went to sleep.

When I woke up, it was morning.

Willy and I raced for the bathroom.
He won.
He must have brushed his teeth
ten times, he took so long.

Nobody was mad at breakfast.
We had blueberry muffins
and Willy got the last one.

After breakfast we had to clear the table.
Willy tried to carry a plate on his head.

The cat got in Willy's way.
He tripped and the plate fell.
It broke into lots of pieces,
and I helped Willy clear up the mess.

Then Willy said, "Want to play horse?"
I said, "All right."
He said, "You be the horse."
Willy used my braids to drive me.
He pulled one braid
if he wanted me to turn.
He pulled both braids
if he wanted me to stop.
That didn't tickle.

When Stewart came over, Willy didn't want to play horse anymore.

I was just as glad.

But now Willy didn't want to play with me anymore either.

He and Stew started building a fort
in the sandbox.

"I want to play," I said.

"No," said Willy.

"It's as much my sandbox as yours,"
I said.

"Oh, you're just a pest," said Willy.

So I kicked over the sand fort.

"Oh, you can have all the sand,"
said Willy. "Come on, Stew."

They climbed a tree that
I couldn't climb.

I went into the house and asked Mommy for three lollipops.

She gave them to me.

"Look, Willy, lollipops!" I called.

"Can I have one?" asked Willy.

"You'll have to come down and get it," I said.

So he came down.

Willy will do anything for a lollipop.

"Want to play marbles?" asked Willy.

"Okay," I said.

"Not you, pest," said Willy.

Willy and Stew played marbles.

I don't like marbles anyway.

I stood behind Stew and I sang,
"Beef stew, chicken stew,
What kind of stew are you, Stew?"
Sometimes I said lamb stew or oyster
stew. I liked my song. I sang my song
over and over again.

But Stew didn't like my song.
"Stop singing that," he said.
"Lamb stew!" I said, and sang louder.
Then he pushed me.
I sat down.
I screamed.
I was so mad.
"Why did you push her?" asked Willy.
" 'Cause she's a pest."
"She is not," said Willy.
"She is too," said Stew.
"You take that back," said Willy.
"She's my sister."
"Okay, okay," said Stew.
"Say she's not a pest. I won't let you up until you do," said Willy.

"Okay, she's not a pest," said Stew. "Now let me up."

Willy let him up.

They shook hands.

"Want to play catch?" asked Willy.

"All right," I said.

"Not you, pest," said Willy.

I was just about to scream again when I saw Allen coming to play with me.

"Hi, Allen," I called. "Let's play lion-
tamer."

"All right," said Allen.

So Allen was the lion,
and he did what I told him to do.